When You Give to a King

Written by: Wes Wesley
Illustrated by: Jasmine Lewis

www.WesBooks.com

ISBN: 978-1-946903-02-0

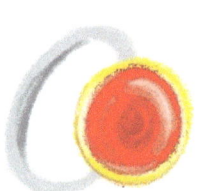

To my wife and kids, Thank you for the
inspiration – W.W.

Once upon a time there was a king, and in his kingdom lived a boy who always gave generously to the people around him.

The people in the kingdom liked the boy because he would always give food to those who were hungry.

The boy also was a great painter. One day he painted a magnificent painting that everyone admired. One man even offered him a great fortune of silver and gold for the painting, but the boy turned down his offer.

The next day the king happen to be riding in his chariot overlooking his kingdom. When the boy saw the king from a distance, he immediately gift wrapped his magnificent painting. As the chariot approached, the boy presented the gift to the king, and the king turned and said, "Thank you."

The boy's family heard what happen and they became upset. They asked him, "Why did you give your painting away for free?" The boy simply said, "When you come into the presence of a king always bring a gift. It puts pressure on the king to out do you in giving!"

When the king got back to his palace, he unwrapped the painting and put it on his bedroom wall.

Two years later the king could not sleep.
So he walked around his bedroom and looked
at the many paintings he had on his wall. When
he came to the painting that the boy gave him,
the king stopped and admired the painting
with a smile.

The king then called his top advisor in his room and asked him, "What did we ever do for the boy who gave me this painting?" The advisor said, "Nothing my lord."

Instantly the king called a meeting with all his top officials. He asked them, "How do you honor a person who gives freely to the king."

The first official said, "Create a parade in his honor."

The second official said, "Let him ride on the king's personal chariot."

The third official said, "Give him a pot of gold."

The king said, "Enough! Let's do all three."

That next morning just as the sun was rising, two of the king's assistants rushed the boy to the palace. He was cleaned up and they dressed him in royal clothes.

Suddenly the king gave the signal and the royal trumpets started to blow. People from all over the kingdom came to the parade as the boy cruised down the street in the king's personal chariot with a pot of gold by his side.

The boy continued to give generously to the people around him all the days of his life, and he lived happily ever after.

End

www.ingramcontent.com/pod-product-compliance
Lightning Source LLC
Chambersburg PA
CBHW041608120626
46551CB00002B/361